TELL ME HOW

HOW DEEP?

by
Azra Limbada

KidHaven PUBLISHING

Published in 2023 by **KidHaven Publishing, an Imprint of Greenhaven Publishing, LLC**
29 East 21st Street
New York, NY 10010

This edition is published by arrangement with Booklife Publishing

Edited by: William Anthony

Designed by: Danielle Webster-Jones

Cataloging-in-Publication Data

Names: Limbada, Azra.
Title: How deep? / Azra Limbada.
Description: New York : KidHaven Publishing, 2023. | Series: Tell me how | Includes glossary and index.
Identifiers: ISBN 9781534540859 (pbk.) | ISBN 9781534540873 (library bound) | ISBN 9781534540866 (6 pack) | ISBN 9781534540880 (ebook)
Subjects: LCSH: Marine animals--Juvenile literature. | Marine ecology--Juvenile literature.
Classification: LCC QL122.2 L563 2023 | DDC 591.77--dc23

Manufactured in the United States of America

CPSIA compliance information: Batch #CSKH23: For further information contact Greenhaven Publishing LLC, New York, New York at 1-844-317-7404.

Please visit our website, www.greenhavenpublishing.com. For a free color catalog of all our high-quality books, call toll free 1-844-317-7404 or fax 1-844-317-7405.

Find us on

Image Credits

Cover - Potapov Alexander, Irina Markova. 4 - Jay Ondreicka. 5 - 3Dstock. 6 - Vlad61. 7 - SpicyTruffel, NoPainNoGain, Rich Carey, Nerthuz, Stock High angle view, Yellow Cat, Alexei Orlov [CC BY (https://creativecommons.org/licenses/by/3.0)], Masaki Miya et al. [CC BY (https://creativecommons.org/licenses/by/2.0)], Lamiot [CC BY (https://creativecommons.org/licenses/by/3.0)], Yulia Kaledina. 8-9 - sciencepics, Valentyna Chukhlyebova, 3DMI, likemuzzy, perori, ibom. 10 - Lerner Vadim. 11 - Poring Studio. 12 - Dotted Yeti. 13 - wildestanimal. 14 - Paul Fleet. 15 - Ase, Mike Goren from New York [CC BY (https://creativecommons.org/licenses/by/2.0)]. 16 - 3DMI, Graphics Master. 17 - Brian Suda from Reykjavík, Ísland [CC BY-SA (https://creativecommons.org/licenses/by-sa/2.0)]. 18 - Silvia Pascual. 19 - Richard Whitcombe. 20 - Ase. 21 - Netfalls Remy Musser. 22 - Flying object. 23 - dwph, Dimonika, Enimados, Monster e. Images are courtesy of Shutterstock.com. With thanks to Getty Images, Thinkstock Photo and iStockphoto.

CONTENTS

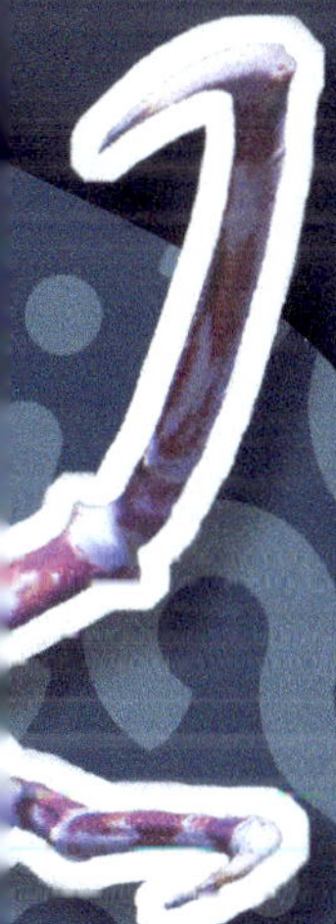

Words that look like <u>this</u> can be found in the glossary on page 24.

EXTREME ANIMALS

Some living things can survive in very **extreme** places. They are called extremophiles. Their homes can be very dangerous, such as the bottom of the ocean.

This red flat bark beetle is an extremophile. It lives in very cold places.

Another extremophile is a tardigrade. They are tiny creatures that can live in both boiling water and freezing temperatures.

A tardigrade is sometimes called a water bear.

LIVING IN THE OCEAN

A habitat is the natural home in which animals, plants, and other living things live. Oceans are one of the largest habitats on Earth.

Did you know that the ocean is split into five layers? The top layer is where you find most sea creatures. The bottom layer is very dark and cold. It is here that you might find some extremophiles.

HOW DEEP?

These animals all live in the ocean. Some live in the lighter and warmer layers, while others live in the deeper, colder layers.

Japanese spider crab

It is the largest known species of crab and can live up to 100 years!

1,000 feet

The Japanese spider crab lives up to 1,000 feet (300 m) below the sea. It has eight legs with two big claws on its front legs.

5,000 feet

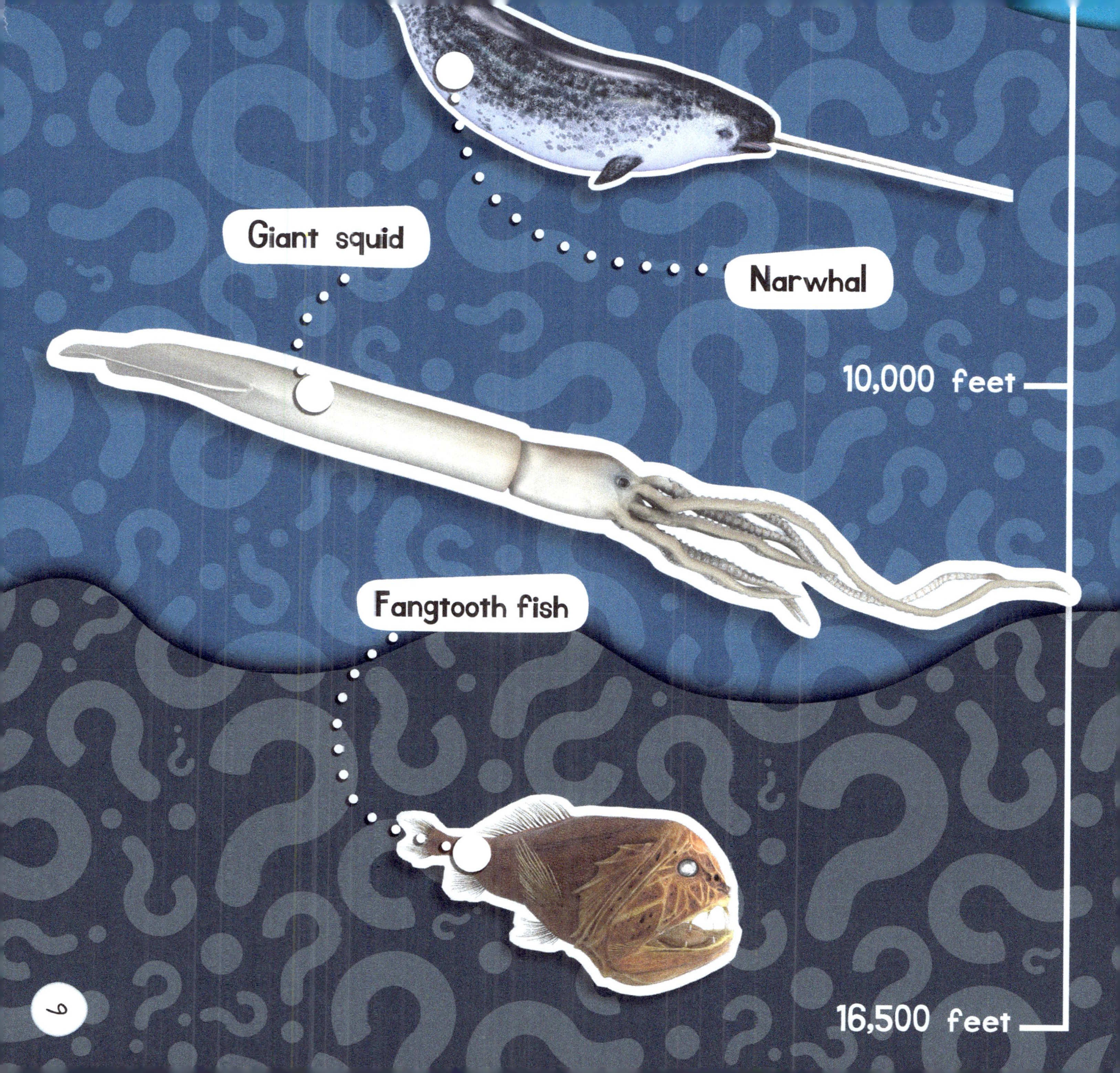
Narwhal
Giant squid
10,000 feet
Fangtooth fish
16,500 feet

JAPANESE SPIDER CRAB

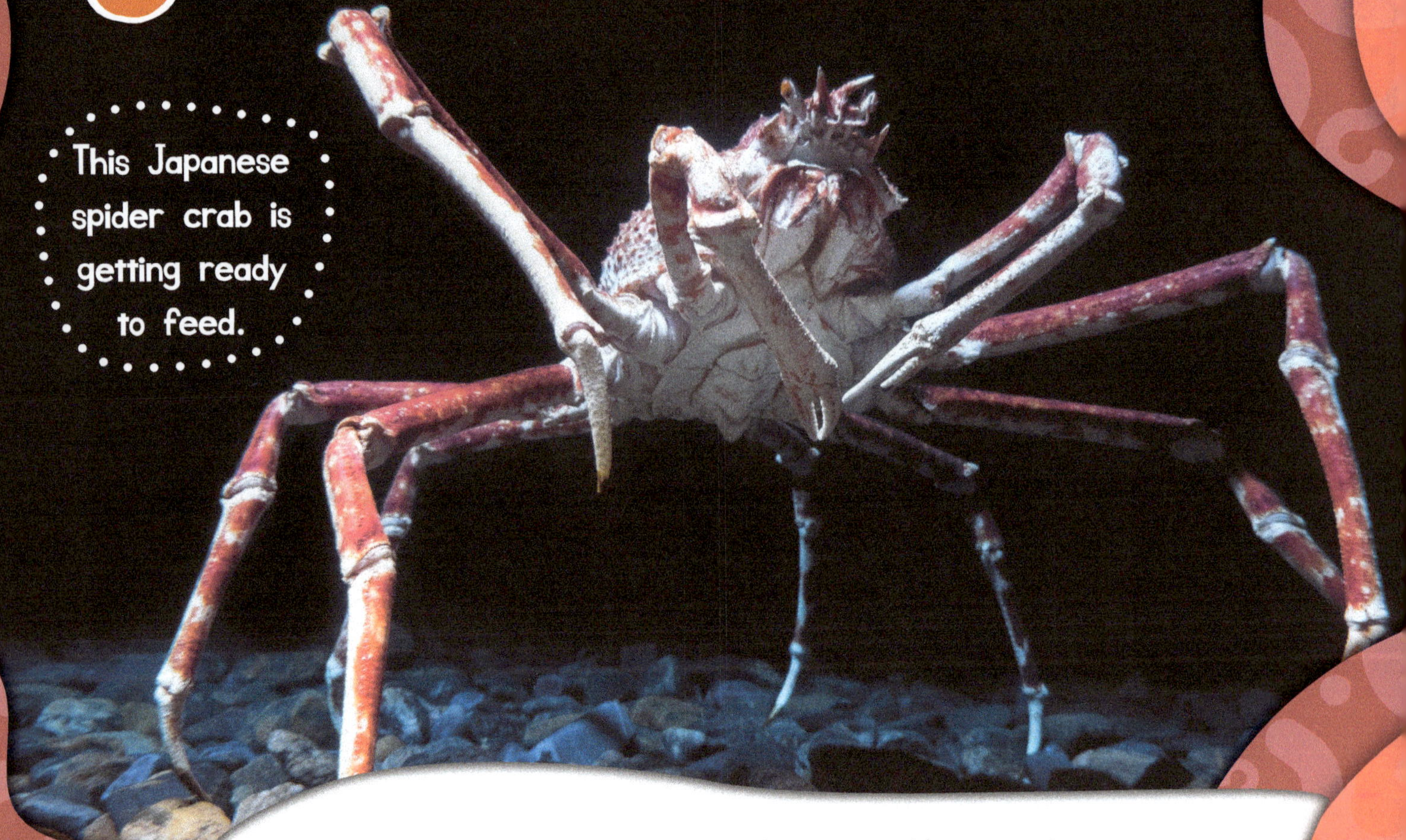

This Japanese spider crab is getting ready to feed.

Japanese spider crabs live in the waters around Japan. They are **scavengers**. They use their giant claws to feed on dead animals.

Japanese spider crabs are thought to be the largest living **arthropods**. They have very long legs and can live up to 100 years.

NARWHAL

The tip of a narwhal's tusk is bendy.

A narwhal is a type of whale. Some narwhals have a long tusk sticking out of their head. Sometimes they are called the unicorns of the sea!

Did you know that the narwhal's tusk is just a long tooth? It can grow up to 10 feet (3 m) long! Narwhals can survive in very cold waters. They live in the **Arctic**.

GIANT SQUID

One of the largest giant squids ever found was 43 feet (13 m) long!

Giant squids are one of the largest known **invertebrates** on Earth. Their eyes are as big as soccer balls! This helps them spot **predators** from far away.

Giant squids can survive in some of the deepest parts of the ocean. They have eight arms and two longer tentacles that they use to feed.

Giant squids might even be able to attack and eat small whales!

FANGTOOTH FISH

Fangtooths like to feed on other fish and squid.

The fangtooth fish lives deep down in the ocean. It has long fangs that it uses to hunt and feed on **prey**.

Fangtooths are dark in color. This means they can blend into the deep, dark ocean. This helps them hide from predators.

Fangtooths are known for liking the dark!

AMAZING ADAPTATIONS

Penguins have lots of fat under their skin to keep them from getting cold.

All animals are adapted to their environment. This means that they have certain **features** that help them to survive in their habitat.

Peacock mantis shrimps are powerful hunters. They catch their prey by punching it. They can move their punching clubs very quickly.

LIFE AT THE BOTTOM OF THE OCEAN

We know more about the moon than we do about the bottom of the ocean, because the ocean is so big and so deep!

The bottom of the ocean is not flat. It has mountains, just like on land. Most animals that live at the bottom of the ocean are extremophiles.

CREATE A CREATURE

Did you know that some deep-sea creatures can make their own light? Some do this to attract prey, while others do it to scare off predators.

This jellyfish can make its own light!

It's your turn to draw a deep-sea creature! Think of how it might be adapted to living at the bottom of the ocean and label all the different parts!

Remember to explain how your creature can survive!

Tip: Give your creature a special name!

GLOSSARY

Arctic the area of the world that includes the North Pole

arthropods a large group of animals with hard shells on the outside of their bodies and no bones inside their bodies

extreme far beyond what is usual or normal

features interesting or important parts

invertebrates animals that do not have a backbone

predators animals that hunt other animals for food

prey an animal that is hunted, caught, and eaten by another animal

scavengers animals that find and feed on dead animals or plants

INDEX